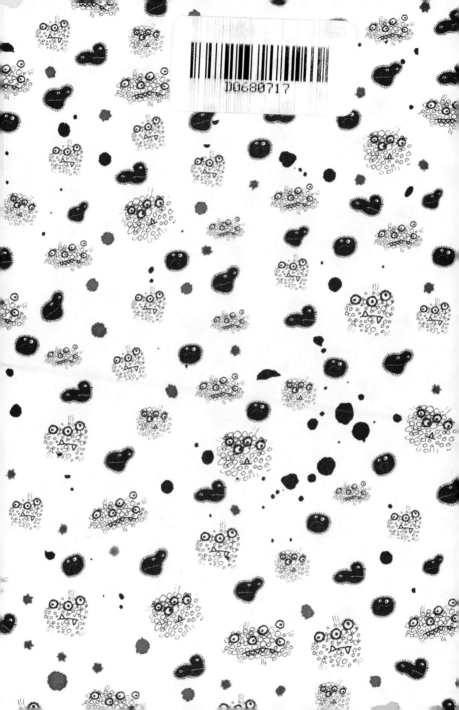

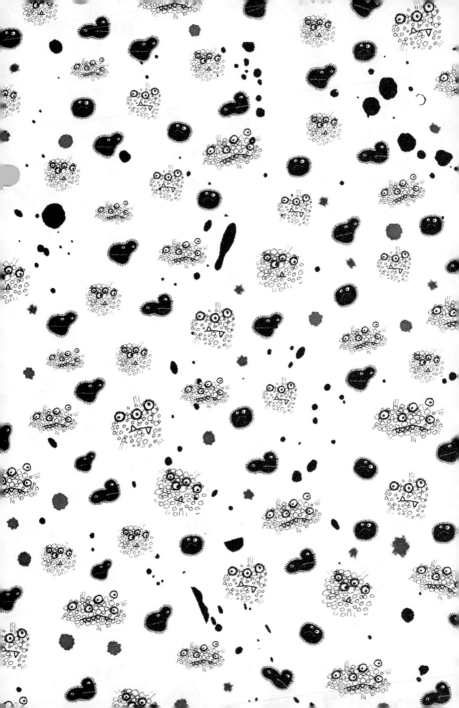

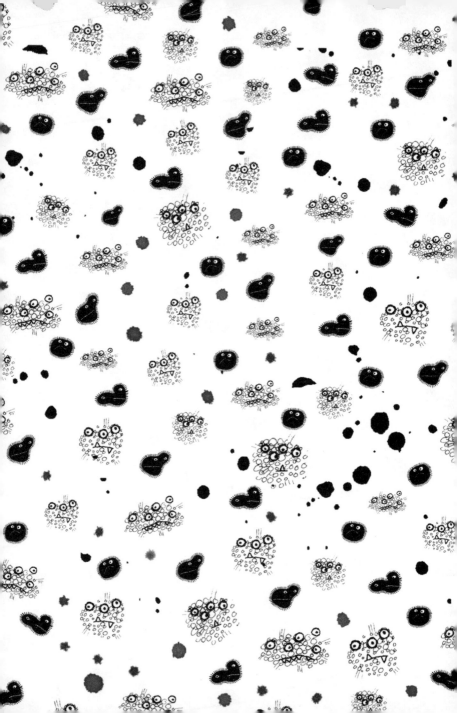

Dirty Bertie

Bertie

GERMS!

DAVID ROBERTS

WRITTEN BY ALAN MACDONALD

CAPSTONE

First published in the United States in 2012
by Stone Arch Books
A Capstone Imprint
1710 Roe Crest Drive
North Mankato, Minnesota 56003
www.capstonepub.com

First published by
Stripes Publishing
1 The Coda Centre, 189 Munster Road
London SW6 6AW

Characters created by David Roberts
Text © Alan MacDonald 2009
Illustrations © David Roberts 2009

Library of Congress Cataloging-in-Publication Data is
available on the Library of Congress website.

ISBN: 978-1-4342-4600-4 (hardcover)
ISBN: 978-1-4342-4266-2 (paperback)

Summary: Bertie tries to catch his sister's chickenpox,
partners with his grandma at a dance competition, and meets
his match in the new babysitter.

Designer: Emily Harris

Photo Credits
Alan MacDonald, pg. 112 ; David Roberts, pg. 112

Printed in the United States of America in Stevens Point, Wisconsin.
042012   006678WZF12

TABLE OF CONTENTS

WARNING!
DON'T BE LIKE BERTIE!
ALWAYS CATCH YOUR
GERMS IN A TISSUE
AND THROW IT AWAY.
AND REMEMBER TO WASH
YOUR HANDS!
IT'S EASY-SNEEZY!

GERMS!

CHAPTER 1

"Are you feeling okay, Suzy?" Mom asked. "You don't look very good."

Bertie looked up from his breakfast. His sister, Suzy, had just drooped into the kitchen.

"I'm hot," Suzy moaned.

"I'm hot too," Bertie said through a mouthful of cereal.

"My head hurts," Suzy croaked. "And I ache all over."

"My head kind of hurts," said Bertie. "It aches when I talk."

Bertie's mom ignored him. "Let me look at you," she said to Suzy. "Goodness! Look at all those spots! I think you have chickenpox."

"Chickenpox?" Suzy said with a groan.

"Chickenpox!" Bertie echoed.

"Yep," Mom said. "You have all the symptoms: small itchy red spots, fever, and aches and pains — sounds like chickenpox to me. You'll have to stay home from school for the whole week."

"The rest of the week?" Bertie exclaimed.

Suzy stuck out her tongue at her brother and drooped back upstairs to bed.

"What about me?" asked Bertie, pulling up his shirt. "I have spots too. Do you think that's chickenpox?"

"I think that's dirt," said Mom. "Now finish your breakfast. And stay away from your sister. Chickenpox is very contagious."

Bertie sighed. It wasn't fair! How come his sister caught chickenpox when he never got anything? If anyone should

be catching something it was him. He
hardly ever washed his hands. And now
Suzy got a whole week off school!

Bertie gulped as he realized what
day it was. Friday — homework day.
As usual, Bertie had avoided doing his
homework until the last minute. As a
matter of fact, he'd forgotten altogether.
But he knew his teacher, Miss Boot,
wouldn't have forgotten.

If only I had chickenpox, thought
Bertie. *That would solve everything.*

Bertie felt his forehead. It did feel
a little hot. He scratched under his
arm. He was definitely itchy. The more
he thought about it, the more he was
convinced he was getting chickenpox
too.

"MOM!" he hollered. "I don't feel good!"

"There's nothing wrong with you," Mom replied. "You just ate two bowls of cereal."

"But that was before," Bertie protested. "Now I feel sick!"

"Don't be ridiculous, Bertie," Mom said. "Now hurry up and brush your teeth. You're going to be late for school."

Bertie stomped upstairs to the bathroom. *No one ever believes me*, he thought. *For all they know, I could be dying!*

Bertie stared at his reflection in the mirror. *Just my luck*, he thought. *Not a single spot.*

Suddenly he remembered what his

mom had said. Chickenpox was very contagious.

Well, that settles it, Bertie thought. *I'll just have to catch it.* After all, why should his sister get to keep it all to herself?

CHAPTER 2

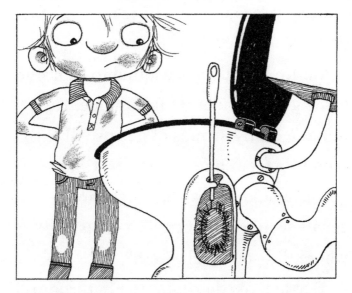

Bertie knew exactly what he needed
to give himself chickenpox — germs.

Germs spread diseases, and luckily
for him, they were everywhere. His
parents were always saying, "Don't
touch that, Bertie, it's covered in germs!"
Cats and dogs had germs. Toilets were

crawling with them. You got germs from picking your nose or eating food off the floor.

Bertie had always wanted to examine some germs under a microscope. He imagined tiny armies of germs, all with scowling faces and hairy legs. Cold germs would be green. Chickenpox germs would be covered in spots. But where did you catch them?

Bertie looked around the bathroom and spotted Suzy's pink toothbrush. That would be covered in her germs!

He squeezed out a blob of toothpaste. Brushing your teeth with your sister's toothbrush was pretty disgusting, even for Bertie, but if it meant missing school it would be worth it.

"Bertie!" called Mom. "What are you doing up there?"

"Nothing!" shouted Bertie. "Just brushing my teeth."

He swallowed some toothpaste to give the germs a better chance to work.

Then he stared at his face in the mirror and waited. But nothing happened.

Unbelievable! Bertie thought. *What do you have to do to catch a few measly germs?*

Bertie walked out of the bathroom

and saw his mom carrying a glass of lemonade down the hall toward Suzy's room.

"Is that for Suzy?" asked Bertie. "Can I take it to her?"

"Why?" Mom asked suspiciously.

"I'm just being helpful," Bertie said sweetly.

"Hmm," said Mom. "I don't think so. I don't want you catching her germs."

"I won't!" said Bertie. "I won't even go near her. I'll just put it down where she can reach it."

Mom eyed Bertie strangely. It wasn't like him to offer to help. "Okay," she said, "but don't spill. And don't bother your sister!"

Bertie smiled to himself. Once Suzy

took a drink from the glass, it would
be covered in her germs! One little sip
of that lemonade, and he'd be drinking
billions of them.

Suzy was sitting up in bed, looking
miserable, when Bertie walked in.

"What do you want?" she groaned.

"I brought you some lemonade," said
Bertie. He smiled sweetly at his sister.

Suzy narrowed her eyes. "Why? What
are you up to?"

"Nothing," said Bertie. "I'm just trying to help."

"You don't fool me," said Suzy. "You want to catch my chickenpox so you don't have to go to school."

"I do not!" Bertie lied. "Have some lemonade!"

"I'm not thirsty," Suzy said.

"Just a sip," Bertie said, holding the glass closer to her.

"Go away!" Suzy yelled.

"Here, let me help," Bertie said. He pressed the glass to Suzy's lips and tipped it up. Suzy choked and spluttered. Lemonade spilled onto her pajamas and the sheets.

"MOM!" wailed Suzy. "BERTIE'S BEING MEAN!"

Mom's feet pounded up the stairs. "What's going on?" she demanded. "Bertie, what did you do?"

"Nothing!" cried Bertie.

"BERTIE SPILLED ON THE BED!" howled Suzy.

"Bertie!" shouted Mom. "GET OUT!"

Bertie quickly escaped to his bedroom. He still had the glass and luckily there was a little lemonade left in the bottom. He could almost see the germs swimming around in it like tiny tadpoles.

Chickenpox, here I come! Bertie

thought. He downed the lemonade
in one big gulp. Then he ran to the
bathroom and stared at his face.

A minute passed. Two minutes. Bertie
lifted his shirt and stared at his belly.
Not a single spot.

This is so unfair, thought Bertie. *Suzy
got chickenpox without even trying!*

Time was running out. Any minute
now, Mom would drag him off to school
and he would have to face Miss Boot.
There was no escape. Unless . . .

Bertie suddenly remembered his
mom's big blue medical book. He raced
into the study and found it on the shelf.
Bertie opened the book and flipped
through its pages. Boils, bruises, burns
. . . there it was — chickenpox!

Chickenpox

Illness common in children.

Symptoms:
Small itchy red spots, fever, aches and pains, sickness, loss of appetite. (see fig. 1)

Treatment:
Bed rest. If a child has chickenpox do NOT send them to school. Even if they beg you.

Bertie read the list of symptoms twice, and then closed the book.

Maybe I don't actually need to catch anything, he thought. *I just need to make Mom think I have chickenpox.*

The more Bertie thought about it, the more brilliant his plan seemed. He'd be completely safe. No Miss Boot, no school, and no handing in homework.

CHAPTER 3

"Bertie, where are you? We need to go!" yelled Mom.

Bertie dragged himself downstairs and slumped into the front hallway. "I'm tired," he moaned.

"Bertie, I don't have time for this," said Mom. "We're already running late,

and I need to hurry and get back to
Suzy. Now let's go."

She opened the front door and
marched off down the driveway.

Bertie dawdled behind at a snail's
pace.

"Bertie, hurry up," Mom said. "You're
going to be late for school."

"I can't hurry up. I'm tired!" moaned
Bertie. "My legs hurt!"

"Bertie," said Mom, "there is nothing
wrong with you! Now let's go!"

"There is too something wrong with
me!" wailed Bertie. "I've got aches and
pains."

"Where?" Mom asked.

"All over," said Bertie.

Mom rolled her eyes. "Bertie, stop.

You're going to school, and that's that. Now let's get going."

She strode off down the road. Bertie followed behind making I'm-going-to-throw-up noises the whole way. But Mom ignored him and kept walking.

"Blech! Urggle!" Bertie sounded as if he was choking.

Mom spun around. "NOW WHAT?"

"I think I'm going to barf!" Bertie said.

"So which one is it, then?" Mom asked. "Your legs hurt, or you're feeling sick?"

"Both," said Bertie. "I think I must be really catching it."

"Catching what?" Mom said, sounding exasperated.

"Suzy's chickenpox!" Bertie exclaimed.

Mom bent down to examine his face. "Chickenpox, huh? So where are the spots?"

Whoops, thought Bertie. He'd completely forgotten about the spots.

Mom folded her arms. "Oh, dear, this is serious," she said. "Very serious.

I know what you've got. It must be homework-itis."

"Um, is that bad?" asked Bertie.

"It's very bad," Mom said. "You catch it when you don't do your homework. There's only one cure, I'm afraid."

"Staying home from school?" Bertie asked hopefully.

"No," said Mom. "Telling your teacher. I'm sure Miss Boot will know what to do. Come on!"

CHAPTER 4

When they reached his school,
Bertie waved to his friends Darren and
Eugene, who were standing out front.
Both of them were holding their finished
homework. Miss Boot prowled around
the playground, glaring at anyone who
dared to make a noise.

Bertie spotted Angela Nunly standing
by the fence and eating a piece of
licorice. Angela lived next door to Bertie.
She was six years old and madly in love
with him. Normally he tried to avoid her,
but right now she was his only chance.

"Is that licorice?" Bertie asked,
walking over to her.

"Yep!" Angela said proudly. "I bought
it with my allowance."

"Can I have a bite?" Bertie asked.

Angela shook her head. "No way! It's
mine!"

"Come on, just a little bit," Bertie
said.

"I've already been chewing on it. It's
got my germs all over it!" said Angela,
waving the soggy licorice.

"I'll trade you my apple," Bertie
offered.

"No, thanks," Angela said.

Bertie didn't have much time. His
mom had finished chatting with Mrs.
Nicely and was getting ready to go.

"I'll give you five dollars for it," he said. "I'll bring it to school on Monday. Promise."

Angela thought about it for a minute. She could buy a lot of licorice with five dollars.

"You promise?" she asked.

"Yes, yes, I promise," Bertie said.

Angela took one last bite of the licorice and handed it over. Bertie immediately popped it in his mouth and started chewing.

His mom walked up right as he swallowed. "Bye, Bertie," she said. "Have a good day at school."

Bertie swallowed. "Mmmmnhh!" he groaned.

"What?" Mom asked. "What is it now?"

Bertie pointed to his throat. "Mmmmnh! Mmmmnh!" he croaked again.

"What? I can't hear what you're saying!" Mom said.

"I said my throat hurts!" Bertie complained.

Mom sighed heavily. "Bertie, we've been through all of this," she said. "There is absolutely nothing wrong with you."

"There is too!" Bertie insisted.

"Okay, fine," Mom said. "Then show me. Open your mouth."

Bertie opened his mouth and stuck out his tongue.

"Oh my goodness!" shrieked Mom. "Your tongue! It's . . . it's BLACK! Why didn't you say something before? We have to get you home immediately!"

The next day, Bertie lay on the couch at home and used the remote to turn on the TV.

He smiled to himself. It was going to be a great day. Suzy felt too sick to leave her bed, so he had the living room all to himself.

He gulped down some more
lemonade and scooped up another giant
bite of chocolate ice cream. Everything
had worked out perfectly.

Mom had wanted to call the doctor
right away, but by the time they got
home, his tongue was looking much
better. Still, she'd decided it was
probably a good idea for him to stay

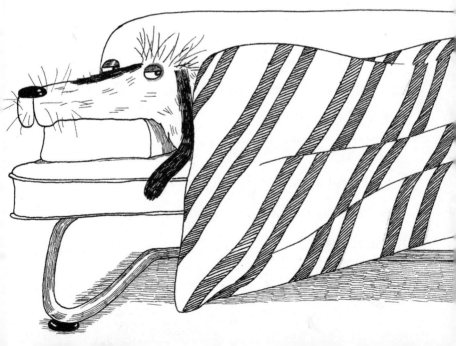

home from school the next day, just to be safe.

Bertie smiled to himself as he took another drink of lemonade. Things had worked out better than he ever could have hoped. He'd managed to avoid facing Miss Boot, and he hadn't even had to catch the chickenpox!

The next morning, Bertie woke up bright and early.

Yes! he thought. *Saturday!* The sun was shining, and he didn't have to go to school. He threw on his clothes and dashed downstairs.

"Oh, you're up," said Mom. "How are you feeling this morning?"

"Way better," said Bertie. "Can I go to the park with Darren and Eugene?"

"No way," said Mom. "I don't want them catching your germs."

Bertie frowned. "But I don't have any germs," he said. "I'm better now. I thought I was catching something, but it turns out I wasn't."

"Oh, really?" said Mom. "Have you looked in the mirror?"

Bertie felt his face. Suddenly he felt itchy. And hot. He dashed into the bathroom and stared at his reflection in the mirror. It couldn't be! It was! His face was covered with hundreds of spots!

STOMP!

CHAPTER 1

Bertie loved Sunday afternoons. His grandma usually stopped by to visit, and she always brought one of her yummy homemade cakes with her. Today she'd brought Bertie's favorite — triple chocolate fudge cake.

"Bertie," said Gran, "what are you doing next Saturday?"

"Nuffink," replied Bertie with his mouth full.

"Well, how would you like to go dancing with me?" Gran asked.

Bertie choked, spraying cake crumbs all over the table. "ME?" he asked.

"Yes," Gran said. "I'm entering a dance competition, and I need a partner. My neighbor Stan usually dances with me, but he hurt his back mowing the lawn."

"But I can't dance!" Bertie exclaimed.

"Of course you can," Gran told him. "You've got two feet."

"And you went to the school dance," Mom pointed out.

"I didn't dance!" said Bertie, horrified.
"I just went for the snacks!"

"Well, I'm sure you'd get the hang
of it with a little practice," Gran said.
"Please, Bertie. For your gran."

Bertie shook his head. There was
no way he was going anywhere near a
dance floor . . . especially not with Gran.

He'd seen the kind of dancing she

was talking about on TV — ballroom dancing! It was all prancing around in tight pants and fluffy skirts.

There's no way she's talking me into this, Bertie thought. *I'd rather eat dog food than dance like that!*

Gran sighed and gave Bertie a sad look. "Oh well," she said. "I guess I'll just have to find someone else to share the prize."

Bertie paused mid-bite. "What prize?" he asked.

"Oh, never mind," Gran said. "I can tell you're not interested."

"Yes I am!" Bertie insisted. "What prize?"

"Well, if we win, the prize is a luxury cruise," Gran told him.

A cruise meant a swimming pool and probably his own servants. Maybe the captain would even let him steer the boat.

"Would I have to miss school?" Bertie asked.

"If you won, I suppose so," said Mom.

"I'll do it!" declared Bertie.

"WOOOO!" yelled Gran. She grabbed Bertie and whirled him around and around the kitchen, until she got dizzy and collapsed into a chair.

Yikes! thought Bertie. *If this is what she calls dancing, we're in big trouble!*

CHAPTER 2

That night, Gran dragged Bertie along to her dance class. He stared in horror at the couples shuffling around the dance floor. Most of them looked older than Egyptian mummies.

Miss Twist, the teacher, stepped forward. She was as tall and thin as a ruler and had her hair scraped into a bun on top of her head.

"How lovely to see a new member," she said. "Let's all give a special welcome to Bertie!"

The class clapped. Bertie doubted anyone would be clapping once they saw him dance.

Miss Twist divided the class up into smaller groups to practice their steps. They started with the waltz.

"And step . . . step . . . slide together," Miss Twist chanted. "Bertie, glide, not stomp! And stop looking at your feet!"

Bertie groaned. This was impossible. How was he supposed to know what his feet were doing if he couldn't look at them?

"One, two, three. One, two, three,"
Miss Twist chanted as the rest of the
class glided around the room like swans.

CLUMP! STOMP! STOMP! CLUMP!
STOMP! STOMP! went Bertie, clomping
like an elephant.

Things got even worse when it was
time to dance with Gran. She was twice

as tall as Bertie, so he found himself
squashed against her chest.

Gran sighed. "Bertie, you're supposed
to be leading!"

"How can I lead if I can't see where
I'm going?" Bertie complained.

Finally it was time for a break.

"Whew, I'm pooped!" Gran wheezed, mopping sweat off her brow. Bertie bought a bottle of water and sat down beside her to rest.

On the dance floor, they watched a tall, elegantly dressed couple practicing their routine. They whirled across the floor as if they were glued together.

"They're really good," said Bertie.

Gran rolled her eyes. "That's Keith and Kerry-Anne, the Southeast Dance Champions, as they never forget to mention. They're the favorites to win on Saturday."

Bertie's mouth dropped open. "You mean we have to beat them?" he asked.

"I'm afraid so," Gran said.

Keith was stamping and waving his arms as if he was trying to take flight.

"What's he doing?" asked Bertie.

"It's a dance called the Paso Doble," Gran explained. "It's like a bullfight."

Bertie's eyes lit up. A bullfight? Now that was his kind of dancing. Much better than a stupid old waltz.

Bertie imagined that he was a famous matador entering the ring. He swept off his red cape and took a bow. The crowd chanted his name. "BERTIE! BERTIE! BERTIE!"

"BERTIE!" hissed Gran, poking him in the ribs.

Bertie looked up to see that the Southeast Dance Champions had stopped dancing and were smiling down at him. Up close, Bertie thought the man's hair looked like a skunk's tail.

Keith reached out and patted Bertie on the head. "Hello, little man. Are you having a good time?"

"I was," Bertie said with a scowl.

Kerry-Anne laid a hand on Gran's arm. "I was so sorry to hear about poor old Stan," she said. "So you won't have a partner for Saturday's competition! Isn't that a shame, Keith?"

Keith yawned. "Yeah, a shame. Still, it's not like you were ever going to win."

"Oh, don't worry," said Gran. "I'm not giving up. In fact, I've already found a new partner, haven't I, Bertie?"

Bertie opened his mouth and let out a loud burp. Keith and Kerry-Anne burst out laughing.

"Hahaha! Oh, that's so adorable!" Kerry-Anne said. "You're going to dance with your grandson! How hilarious!"

Gran folded her arms. "I don't see

what's so funny," she snapped. "Bertie happens to be an excellent dancer. Isn't that right, Bertie?"

"Yep," said Bertie. "And I've watched it on TV."

"Then you probably know we've been crowned the Southeast Dance Champions three years in a row," boasted Keith. "Our Paso Doble is legendary!"

"Huh!" said Bertie. "We're doing the Passo Doobie too, aren't we, Gran?"

Gran's eyebrows nearly hit the ceiling.

"You?" scoffed Keith. "You couldn't dance the Hokey Pokey! Come on, Kerry-Anne, let's leave these amateurs to their dreams."

As soon as Keith and Kerry-Anne had

disappeared, Bertie nudged Gran. "Did
you see that?" he said. "He's wearing a
wig!"

"Never mind that," Gran said. "Why
did you tell them we're going to dance
the Paso Doble?"

Bertie shrugged. "It just came out.

What's the big deal? I thought you wanted to win?"

"I do!" Gran said. "But the Paso Doble takes months of practice!"

Bertie gulped the rest of his drink. "Well, then, we'd better get started," he said.

CHAPTER 3

For the rest of the week, Bertie practiced every chance he got. He was determined to win the contest. No way were creepy Keith and Kerry-Anne winning that luxury cruise.

Bertie threw himself into learning to dance like a matador. He practiced his steps in his bedroom, stomping up

and down on the floor until his dad finally yelled at him to be quiet. He even practiced on his way to school, which earned him a lot of funny looks from people at the bus stop.

On Friday, Mom found Bertie having a tug-of-war with Whiffer, the family dog, in the kitchen.

"Bertie! What on earth are you doing?" she cried.

"Practicing!" panted Bertie.

Mom took a closer look. "Is that my favorite scarf?" she yelled.

"I just borrowed it," Bertie said. "I needed it for my costume."

"Get it out of the dog's mouth!" Mom hollered.

"I'm trying!" Bertie gasped. "He won't . . . let . . . go!"

There was the sound of something ripping. Whiffer let go.

"Phew!" puffed Bertie, sitting down. "Dancing is hard work."

The day of the contest finally arrived.
The finals were being held at the
Regency Ballroom. Bertie's whole family
was coming, even though he'd begged
them to stay away. His sister, Suzy, said
she wouldn't miss it for the world.

Gran and Bertie had to stop at the
costume store along the way to pick
up their costumes for the Paso Doble.
Gran's dress was a Spanish flamenco
dress covered with bright red polka dots.
Unfortunately, it was made for someone
a lot smaller than she was.

Bertie stood outside the changing

rooms, waiting while she wrestled with
the zipper.

"You'll have to suck it in," panted the
shop assistant.

"I AM sucking it in!" Gran said.

Bertie was already wearing his
matador's costume with a black hat
and a scarlet cape. He stood in front
of a tall mirror, swirling the cape like a
bullfighter.

"Olé! Olé! Ol-oops!" Bertie said.

A stack of boxes toppled off the
counter. He quickly bent down to
pick them up. The boxes were full of
things like ice-cube flies and whoopee
cushions. Most interesting of all was a
small red box labeled "Itching Powder."

Bertie's eyes lit up. Think what you

could do with itching powder! You could
use it on someone you didn't like. Like
Keith or Kerry-Anne, for instance.

That's not a bad idea, Bertie thought.
It might even help us win the contest.

Without a second thought, Bertie
slipped the box into his pocket and left
some money on the counter.

CHAPTER 4

When Gran and Bertie arrived at the
Regency Ballroom, the audience was
already seated. Bertie and Gran hurried
backstage to get ready.

While Gran pinned up her hair in
front of the mirror, Bertie looked around
the room. This was his chance.

He set off in search of their rivals. He found Kerry-Anne in her private dressing room, wearing a poofy skirt and a scowl.

"What do you think you're doing?" she snapped.

"Oh, sorry, I was, um . . . looking for Gran," said Bertie.

"She's not here," said Kerry-Anne. "But since you've barged in, you can make yourself useful. Go get my dress for me — the blue one with the sequins. It's hanging on the rack in the hallway."

Bertie grinned. This was too good a chance to miss. He walked back into the hall and saw the dress hanging on a rack.

Checking to make sure no one was

watching, Bertie pulled the red box out of his pocket.

Suddenly, Keith's laughter boomed from the next room. "Haha! It's hilarious! The kid hardly comes up to her waist!"

That did it. Bertie shook some of the orange powder into the lining of Kerry-Anne's dress. It wouldn't take long to work — *then* they'd see who was hilarious.

"Ladies and gentlemen, please welcome our dancers to the floor for the Paso Doble!"

This is it, thought Bertie nervously. His costume was making him sweat. Worse still, his cape was so long that he kept tripping on it.

"Bertie, we're on!" Gran whispered, pushing him forward. Bertie stumbled out onto the dance floor. Gran skidded into the spotlight after him, grabbing Bertie to keep her balance.

The audience giggled. In the front row, Bertie could see Mom, Dad, and Suzy trying not to laugh.

The music started. Keith, Kerry-Anne, and the other couples started dancing, weaving patterns across the floor.

Bertie swirled his red cape around
and around. He was a fearless matador.
STOMP! STOMP! went his feet.
SWISH! SWISH! went his cape.

STOMP! SWISH! ARGH! The cape went right over his head.

Bertie stumbled about blindly, trying to get it off.

"Ow!" He collided with something soft. It was Gran, and the two of them wobbled unsteadily. Gran stepped on the train of her dress and fell over. Bertie landed on top of her.

"LOOK OUT!" cried one of the other dancers, but it was too late.

CRAAAAASH!

THUMP!

THUD!

Bertie pushed his matador's hat off of his eyes. Dancers lay in a messy tangle of arms, legs, bows, and ruffles in the middle of the dance floor. Bertie climbed

off Gran, who had gotten stuck in the pile of struggling dancers.

A judge was marching toward them with a clipboard in his hands and an angry expression on his face.

Bertie gulped. He had a feeling his dancing days were over.

Gran and Bertie sat on the sidelines, watching the final round of the dance competition. They were done dancing — the judges had disqualified them as a danger to other contestants.

"Oh, well," said Gran. "We did our best. I'm sorry we won't be going on that cruise, Bertie."

"It's okay," Bertie said with a shrug.

"It's just a shame those two show-offs are going to win again," Gran said. She pointed to where Keith and Kerry-Anne were whirling across the floor. "They'll be bragging about it for weeks. Look at them!"

Bertie watched as Keith lifted Kerry-Anne over his head. Her shoulders twitched.

"I wouldn't be so sure about that," Bertie said. "Maybe things are just warming up."

Kerry-Anne was starting to act very strangely. She was wriggling around like she had ants in her pants. Bertie giggled to himself. The itching powder was starting to work.

"What's wrong with you?" hissed Keith.

"I can't help it!" Kerry-Anne whispered back. "It's this dress. It's so itchy!" She scratched at her back.

"Stop that!" snapped Keith. "People are staring! Pull yourself together!"

"I'm trying!" squealed Kerry-Anne.
"But . . . eeek! Argh! It itches!"

She stamped her feet and pawed at
her arms. She scratched her back like
a dog with fleas. Keith tried to grab her
hands, but she shook him off.

"DON'T JUST STAND THERE!"
she yelled. "DO SOMETHING! I'M ON
FIRE!"

Keith did what you do when
something is on fire. He grabbed a bottle
of water from the nearest table and
emptied it over his partner's head.

There was a brief, terrible silence.
Then Kerry-Anne started screaming.

"ARGHHH! YOU . . . YOU . . .
IDIOT!" she yelled. She swiped at Keith,
pulling his hair right off his head.

Keith gasped and turned bright red. Clutching his bald head, he fled from the dance floor.

"See!" shouted Bertie. "I told you it was a wig!"

The audience cheered. If this was ballroom dancing, they wanted more.

Gran was laughing so hard she had tears streaming down her face. "Well," she said, "that was the best show I've seen in years. I wonder what got into Kerry-Anne?"

Bertie smiled innocently. "Maybe she just had an itch," he suggested.

Things hadn't worked out so badly after all. He wouldn't be going on a cruise, but at least he still had the itching powder. And there was plenty left in the box.

I wonder if Miss Boot can dance, Bertie thought. *Only one way to find out. . . .*

CHAPTER 1

Mom put down the phone. "That was Gran. She can't come."

"What?" Dad said. "What do you mean she can't come? She's babysitting tonight!"

"She was," Mom said. "But she went to the doctor today because she didn't feel well. She has the flu."

Dad groaned. "What are we going to do now? Paul and Penny are expecting us."

Bertie looked up from the comic he was reading. "It's okay," he said. "I can take care of myself."

It would be great not having a babysitter. His sister, Suzy, was sleeping over at her friend's house, so he would have the house all to himself. It would be a great night — eating junk food, watching TV, and staying up late. Gran was a terrible babysitter anyway. She always fell asleep in the middle of playing pirates.

Bertie sighed. He didn't see why he needed a babysitter. It wasn't like he was a baby. He knew where the snacks were and how to work the TV, so he'd be just fine.

Mom didn't agree. "Don't be ridiculous, Bertie," she said. "We can't possibly leave you on your own."

"Why not?" asked Bertie.

"What if something happened?" Mom said.

"Like what?" Bertie asked.

"Like you burning down the house," said Dad.

Mom sighed. "I'll just have to call Penny and cancel."

"But we canceled on them the last time," said Dad. "There has to be someone who can babysit. What about Alice?"

"She's back at college," Mom said.

"How about Jackie?" Dad suggested.

"There's no way she'll come," Mom said. "Not after Bertie put a slug in her hair."

"It wasn't a slug!" Bertie protested. "It was a snail!"

Mom ignored him. "I know!" she said. "What about Kevin?"

Bertie looked up. Kevin? Mean Kevin from across the street? He'd barely ever said two words to Bertie! Were Mom and Dad crazy? Bertie would rather do his homework all night than spend an evening with Kevin!

"Does Kevin babysit?" asked Dad, doubtfully.

"It's worth a try," Mom said. "I'll call over there and find out."

Five minutes later, it was all settled.

"Kevin is on his way," announced Mom.

"Oh, great," Bertie said bitterly. "Don't worry about me! You two just go out and leave me with Frankenstein. I'm sure I'll be fine."

"Bertie, Kevin is just a normal teenager," said Mom. "He's probably shy!"

"He doesn't look shy to me," said Bertie darkly. "He looks like a murderer."

"Besides, it'll be nice to have a boy to babysit for a change," said Mom. "Maybe you two can play a game together."

Bertie scowled. He hated having babysitters. And Kevin was going to be the worst ever.

CHAPTER 2

DING DONG!

Mom hurried to the front door to let
Kevin in.

"Kevin! How are you?" she said.
"Come on inside. Bertie's in the
living room. He's so excited you're
babysitting!"

Kevin drooped into the living room
and flopped into a chair. He looked like
he was going to a funeral. He wore black
jeans, a black T-shirt with a picture of
a skull on it, and a long black coat. He
stared at Bertie through a curtain of
dark hair.

"Okay, we'd better get going," said

Mom brightly. "Don't stay up too late, Bertie."

"And DON'T make a mess," added Dad.

With that, Bertie's parents hurried out of the house, slamming the door behind them.

A heavy silence filled the room. Bertie picked his nose. He stared at Kevin and waited for him to tell him to stop. But Kevin just sat there like a dark cloud.

Bertie looked at the ceiling and let out a loud burp. He glanced at Kevin. Kevin looked bored to death.

Bertie put his feet up on the coffee table. Kevin let out a loud yawn and rolled his eyes.

Bertie couldn't understand it. Most of

his babysitters started yelling at him in the first five minutes.

Bertie glanced around the room for something to do next. "I'm hungry," he announced.

Kevin just stared at him.

"Mom usually lets me have a snack when she goes out," Bertie said. "Can I get one?"

Kevin shrugged. "Whatever."

Great! thought Bertie. Normally he had to wait until bedtime before he got a snack — and even then it was only one tiny cookie. But Kevin didn't seem to care what he did.

Bertie hurried into the kitchen. He eyed the cupboard where Mom kept all the good snacks. He wasn't allowed to

snoop in there. The last time he'd gotten
in there, he'd made himself sick eating
a king-size candy bar. Mom had banned
him from there ever since.

But one tiny little snack won't hurt,
Bertie thought. *Mom will never even find
out.* He opened the cupboard and peered
inside.

CREAAAK!
The door
opened
behind
him.

Bertie
jumped,
banging his
head on the
counter and

dropping the bag of chips he'd grabbed out of the cupboard.

When he turned around, Kevin was standing in the doorway watching him. It was creepy how he could appear without making a sound.

"Oh, um . . . hi," said Bertie. "I was just uh . . . getting some chips."

"Yeah?" said Kevin.

"Do you want some?" Bertie offered.

Kevin shrugged. "If you want."

"Okay, what flavor?" asked Bertie. "We've got plain, barbecue, or sour cream and onion."

Kevin took all three.

CRUNCH! CRUNCH! CHOMP!

Bertie watched in amazement as Kevin wolfed down all the chips. He chewed with his mouth open. He slurped and burped and dropped crumbs on the carpet.

And Mom and Dad say I'm a messy eater, thought Bertie. *Obviously they've never seen Kevin.*

"Had enough?" asked Bertie.

Kevin didn't answer. Instead, he dropped the empty chip bags on the floor.

"We've got cookies," Bertie offered.

"Yeah?" said Kevin.

"In the cookie jar," Bertie told him. "Or there's chocolate bars, but Mom notices if they're missing."

"Yeah?" Kevin said.

"Yeah." Bertie thought it over. "But I guess one would be okay," he said.

CHAPTER 3

BUUUUURP!

Kevin wiped a smear of chocolate
from around his mouth. Bertie lay back
on the sofa and patted his full stomach.
To tell the truth, he was feeling a little
sick.

The living room floor was littered
with chip bags, chocolate bar wrappers,
and cookie crumbs. Kevin glanced at the
clock.

Uh oh, thought Bertie. It was almost
nine o'clock — way past his bedtime.
But maybe Kevin didn't know that.

"Mom usually lets me stay up late on
Saturdays," Bertie fibbed.

"Yeah?" Kevin asked.

"Yeah, when I have a babysitter it's
fine," Bertie said.

Kevin shrugged. "Whatever," he
replied.

Bertie could hardly believe his luck.
His mom and dad never let him stay up
later than nine o'clock — not even on
Christmas Eve!

If I keep Kevin busy, I bet I could stay up all night! Bertie thought.

"Do you want to play a game?" he asked Kevin.

Kevin scratched a spot on his chin. Bertie wondered how he managed to see anything through all that hair.

"Not like a board game," said Bertie. "We could play something cool. Like pirate ships. Or alien invasion. Or maybe have a pillow fight?"

Kevin stopped scratching.

WHACK! THUMP!
Bertie whacked Kevin as hard as he

could with a pillow. Kevin thwacked
him back. Together they bounced up
and down on the couch, smacking each
other with pillows.

This is great, thought Bertie. *Kevin is
the best babysitter ever!*

Mom never let him have pillow fights
or jump on the sofa. She always said
something would get broken.

WHUMP!

Bertie swung his pillow back behind
him, hitting a lamp. The lamp tipped
over and knocked into a vase of flowers.
The vase wobbled back and forth for a
second before falling to the floor with a
loud *CRASH!*

"Whoops!" said Bertie.

WHUMP! Kevin's pillow walloped

Bertie in the face. The pillow ripped open, filling the room with clouds of feathers.

THUMP! CLUMP! WHAM! WHAP!

Out of breath, Kevin and Bertie flopped back on the sofa.

"Phew," panted Bertie. "That was great. What should we do now?"

Kevin didn't respond. Instead, he picked up the remote and turned on the TV.

This is the life, thought Bertie. Mom and Dad never let him watch TV this late at night. And there were so many great shows he wanted to see.

Bertie grabbed the remote from Kevin and flipped through the channels. A love story — yuck! A cooking show — boring! A game show, a commercial, more commercials, a horror movie . . .

Wait a second! Bertie quickly flipped back. He never got to watch scary movies.

"Should we watch this?" he asked Kevin.

For the first time all night, Kevin looked interested. *"Night of the Zombies III*. Cool!" he said. "It's really scary."

It turned out that Kevin had seen lots of scary movies. It was the first time Bertie had heard him say more than

three words. They turned off the lights
and settled down to watch the film.

In the movie, it was midnight. The
moon was out. The people in the house
were all asleep. An eerie mist rose off the
lake.

Bertie sank deeper and deeper into

the sofa. He hugged his pillow. He hoped
there weren't any zombies in this film.

THUD, THUD, THUD!

Bertie gulped. The zombies were
coming.

CRASH! A zombie's hand smashed
through a window.

"YEAARRRRGH!" Bertie yelped. He jumped up and dove behind the sofa. He peered out at the TV screen from his hiding place.

The zombies were in the house now. They walked like robots and had blank, staring eyes. They climbed up the stairs to where the unsuspecting people were sleeping. . . .

Bertie bit his fingernails nervously. Why hadn't anyone warned him scary movies were so . . . scary?

Maybe I should go to bed, Bertie thought. But he knew if he went upstairs, he'd never be able to fall asleep. He would lie there, all alone, in his room in the dark. And what if the zombies came to get him?

Bertie snuck another glance at the TV screen through his fingers.

Suddenly, two bright eyes shone through the front curtains like headlights, illuminating the living room.

Wait a moment, Bertie thought. *Those are headlights.* A car was pulling into the drive.

Oh, no! This was worse than any scary movie! Mom and Dad were home early!

CHAPTER 4

Bertie looked around the living room frantically. The house looked like a tornado had gone through it. The floor was a sea of chip bags, cookie crumbs, and sticky chocolate wrappers. There was a wet spot on the carpet where the flowers had spilled, and beside it were the remains of Mom's favorite vase.

One of the pillows looked like a balloon that had been popped. White feathers had settled on everything like snow.

Bertie felt a wave of panic. If Mom and Dad saw the house like this, he was dead!

He grabbed Kevin by the arm. "Hurry up!" he hollered. "They're back!"

"What?" Kevin asked, sounding confused. "Who's back?"

"My mom and dad!" Bertie yelled. "We have to clean up!"

Kevin just frowned at him. "Sit down! You're blocking the screen. This is a good part!"

Bertie couldn't believe it. Was Kevin just going to sit there and watch the movie? This was a matter of life and death!

A car door slammed. Any minute now Dad's key would turn in the lock. There was no time to lose.

Bertie flew around the room like a whirlwind. He hid the torn pillows behind the TV. He brushed feathers under the sofa. He picked up the fallen lamp and frantically dabbed at the puddle on the carpet with tissues.

What else? What else? Bertie thought. *Mom's favorite vase!*

He got down on his hands and knees and picked up the broken pieces. While he was down there, he quickly grabbed

flowers and chip bags and sticky
wrappers.

THUD! THUD! THUD!

They were coming up the path! Bertie
rushed into the kitchen with his arms

full. Quick, quick! Where could he hide
the evidence?

Bertie's eyes fell on the refrigerator.
Perfect! No one would look in there! He
yanked open the fridge door and stuffed
everything inside.

RATTLE, RATTLE! That was Dad's
key turning in the lock.

Bertie slammed the refrigerator door
closed and thumped up the stairs in a

blur of speed. He burst into his room and dove under the covers as fast as he could.

"Kevin! We're back!" Bertie heard Mom call. "Was everything okay? Did Bertie listen to you?"

Just in time! Bertie thought as he lay in bed panting. He listened with his heart pounding as Mom and Dad talked to Kevin.

A few minutes later, he heard the front door slam. Kevin was gone. Bertie lay back and breathed a sigh of relief. That had been a close call, but he'd gotten away with it. Mom and Dad hadn't noticed anything.

Bertie snuck out of bed and crept to the top of the stairs.

"That Kevin is such a nice, quiet boy," Mom was saying. "I hope he and Bertie got along okay."

"Well, at least Bertie's in bed," said Dad. "And the house is still in one piece. That's progress. Do you want a bedtime drink?"

Bertie froze. No! How could he have been so stupid? His dad always made hot chocolate at bedtime. And hot chocolate needed milk. And milk was kept in the . . .

CRASH!
CLATTER!
SMASH!

"BERTIE!"

When he was young, **Alan MacDonald** dreamed of becoming a professional soccer player, but when he  won a pen in a writing competition, his fate was sealed. Alan is now a successful author and television writer and has written several award-winning children's books, which have been translated into many languages.

David Roberts worked as a fashion illustrator in Hong Kong before turning to children's books. He has worked with a long list of  writers, including Philip Ardagh, Georgia Byng, Carol Ann Duffy, and Chris Priestley. David has also won a gold award in the Nestle Children's Book Prize for *Mouse Noses On Toast* in 2006, and was shortlisted for the 2010 CILIP Kate Greenaway medal for *The Dunderheads*.

Read more about Bertie at
capstonekids.com/characters/dirty-bertie

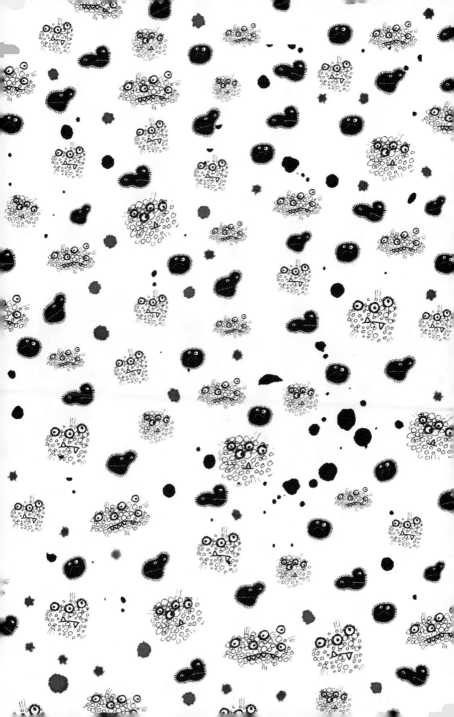

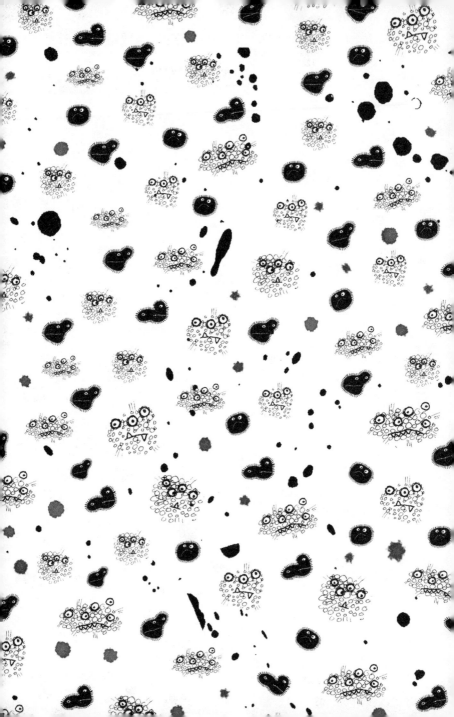

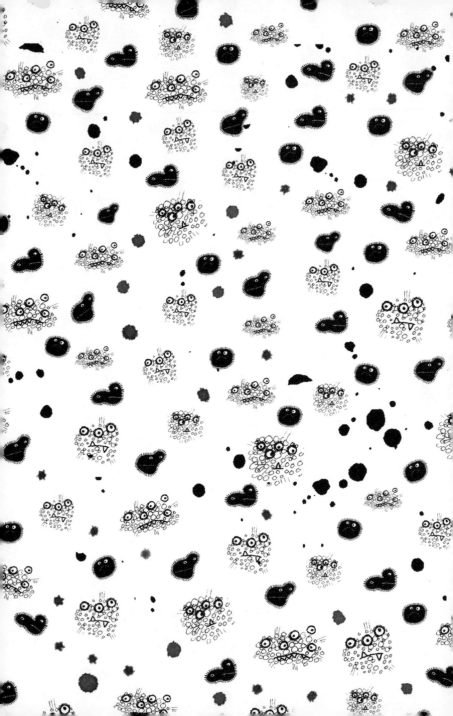